Written and Illustrated by:
Mike Boldt

CreativeKiDs
p u b l i s h i n g

ISBN 978-1-55454-452-3

Copyright © 2008 Creative Kids Publishing, a division
of Transglobal Communications Group, Inc.
5550 Skylane Boulevard, Suite G
Santa Rosa, CA 95403

November is a very
important time of
the year at the North Pole.
Christmas is starting to draw
near and Santa Bearclaws
has his list all done and ready,
but the important task of
checking it twice remains.
Santa checks the list the first
time, while it is Leonard's job
as head elf to do the second
and final check.

"Amy... check?" Santa starts.

"Amy... double checked,"
Leonard replies.

"Andrew... check."

"Andrew... double checked."

And on it goes over many many days until the entire list has been checked twice. This year, however, Leonard was starting to act funny after only a few hours until something finally happened shortly into the B's.

"Becky... check."

"... Becky... checked and double checked **AGAIN** and **AGAIN**. Checked **ONCE** checked **TWICE, ALWAYS THE SAME—NEVER A MISTAKE!**" Leonard exploded.

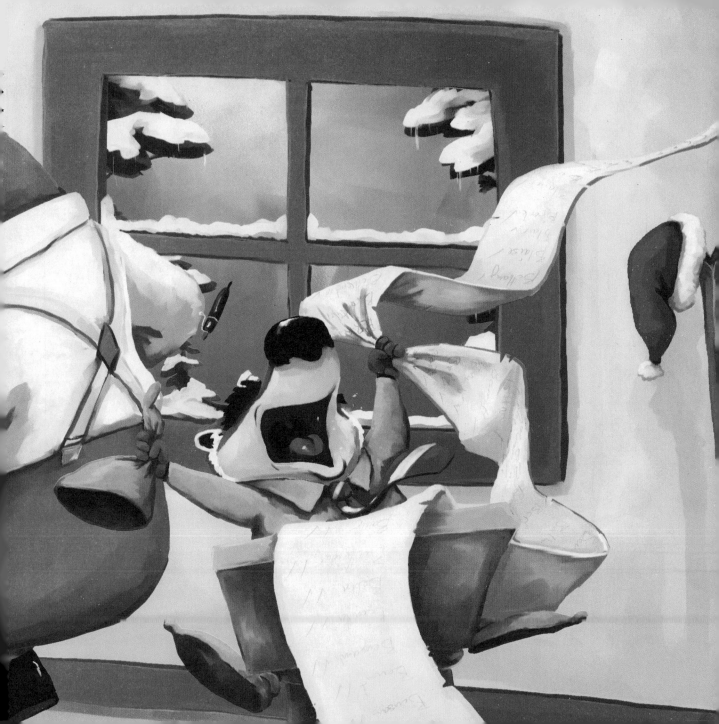

"Leonard! Is everything alright?" asked Santa Bearclaws.

The frazzled head elf sat huffing and puffing in a sort of confused, frustrated, and exhausted slump.

"S..s..sir," he finally said. "Every year you check the list and then I double check it. And every year, I double check it for no reason because you never make any mistakes, and it is making me crazy! I think I would be more useful doing another job."

"Well, maybe you don't need to be the elf checking it twice then," Santa said. "You have been working really hard here Leonard and I am sure we could find one of the other elves to help me with this."

"Well, I guess that would be okay," Leonard agreed.

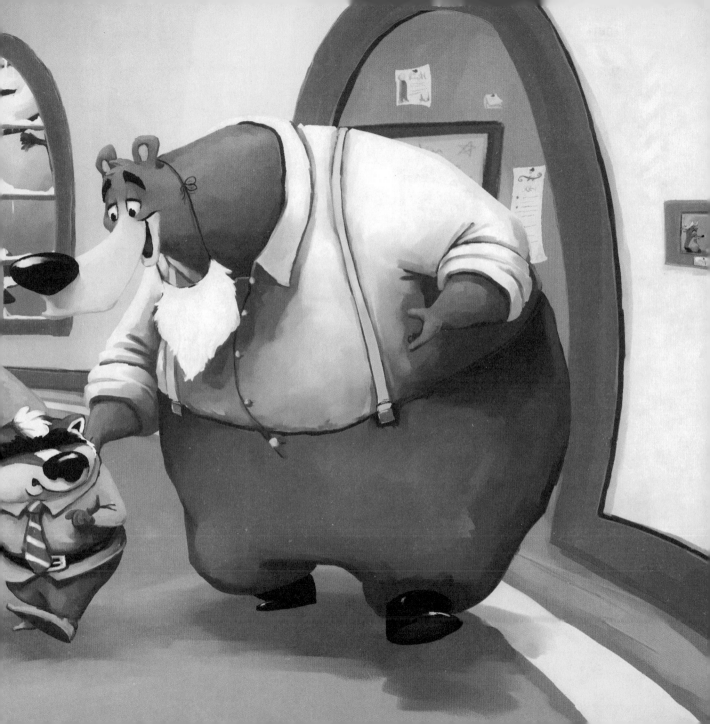

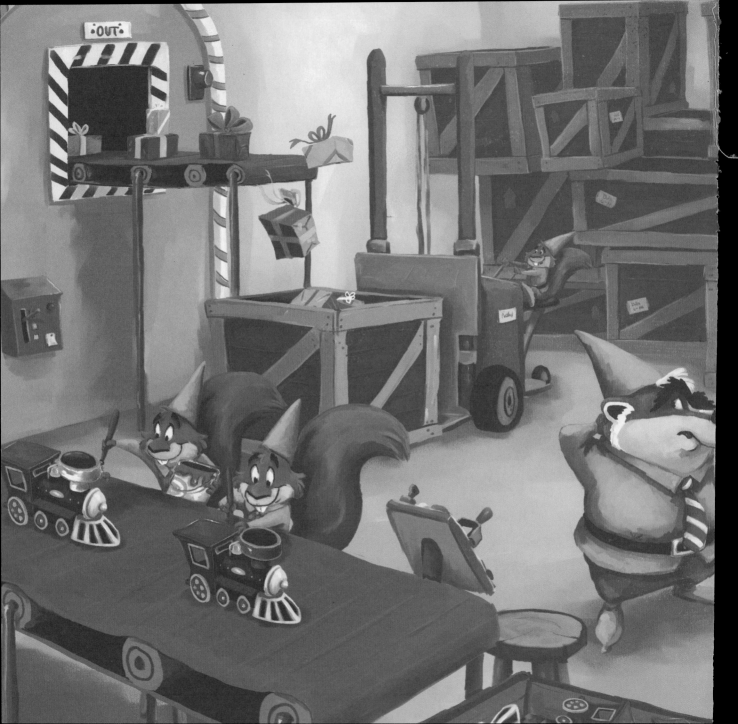

So Leonard returned to the main toy assembly line among the other elves. He found everything working smoothly and so there was actually not that much for him to do.

He created new ways to make the factory even more efficient, but this created even less work for him. Soon Leonard was just wandering around pretending to work and look busy.

Meanwhile, Santa was now checking the list only once. The elf who had replaced Leonard was a little too enthusiastic and was more of a hindrance than a help.

The three elves after him were the same. So Santa, now a bit behind, decided it would be best to just leave the elves out and do it himself.

A few weeks had passed into December. Leonard had exhausted all his efforts to improve work all over the North Pole. One night, he found himself walking aimlessly through the halls of the office. As he passed by Santa's office, he noticed the light had been left on and peeked in to find it empty.

"I wonder how Santa has been doing with the list?" he muttered to himself as he walked slowly over to the desks.

"Surely it wouldn't hurt for me to just double check the page Santa has here on top." So Leonard skimmed over the short list of names without much interest. But then something caught his eye near the bottom!

Leonard had to take a second look to believe it. But somewhere in Santa's efforts to complete the list all on his own, he had forgotten to include the S's on the list. It went straight from "Ryan" to "Taylor"!

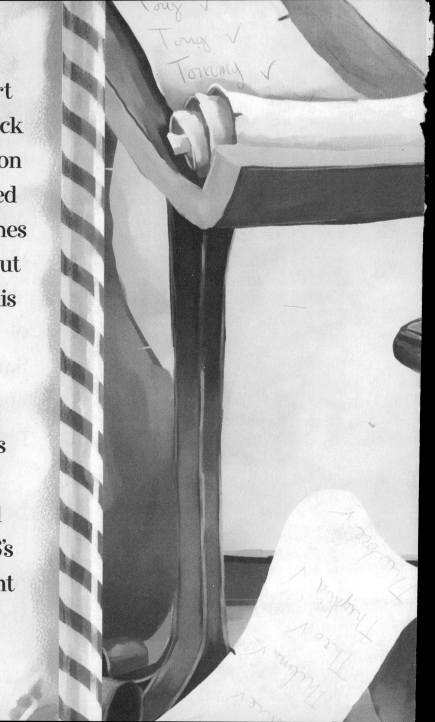

Early the next morning, Santa Bearclaws came into the office to find Leonard hard at work. "Hey Leonard, what are you doing here?"

"Sorry sir, but I just kind of stumbled onto a mistake on the list last night and had to fix it. Somewhere along the line the S's got left out."

"Oh my," gasped Santa. "That would have been disastrous. You saved Christmas this year Leonard!"

"Well, actually sir, it was me checking it again after you had finished with it," Leonard explained. "Checking it twice saved this mistake from happening. Would you mind if I came back to help you check over the list sir?"

"Of course not, I would love that," Santa beamed. "Who knows, maybe next year we should check it three times; the reindeer could help next time."

They both looked serious as they thought about it, then burst out laughing.

"Ummm, I think twice is enough, sir."